Zoey
AND
SASSAFRAS
DRAGONS AND MARSHMALLOWS

THE
INNOVATION
PRESS

READ THE REST OF THE SERIES

for activities and more visit
ZOEYANDSASSAFRAS.COM

TABLE OF CONTENTS

FOR TIM — ML
FOR GOOSE AND BUBS — AC

Publisher's Cataloging-in-Publication
Citro, Asia, author.
Dragons and marshmallows / Asia Citro ; illustrator, Marion Lindsay.
pages cm -- (Zoey and Sassafras ; 1)
Summary: A girl, Zoey, and her cat, Sassafras, use science experiments to help a dragon with a problem.
Audience: Grades K-5.
LCCN 2016904046
ISBN 978-1-943147-08-3; ISBN 978-1-943147-09-0; ISBN 978-1-943147-10-6;
ISBN 978-1-943147-11-3; ISBN 978-1-943147-12-0
1. Cats--Juvenile fiction. 2. Dragons--Juvenile fiction. [1. Cats--Fiction. 2. Dragons--Fiction.
3. Science--Experiments--Fiction. 4. Experiments--Fiction.] I. Lindsay, Marion, illustrator. II.
Title. III. Series: Citro, Asia. Zoey and Sassafras ; 1.
PZ7.1.C577Dr 2016
[E]
QBI16-600078

Text copyright 2017 by Asia Citro
Illustrations copyright 2017 by Marion Lindsay
Journal entries handwritten by S. Citro

Published by The Innovation Press
1001 4th Avenue, Suite 3200, Seattle, WA 98154
www.theinnovationpress.com

Printed and bound by Worzalla
Production Date: September 2020 | Plant Location: Stevens Point, Wisconsin

Cover design by Nicole LaRue | Book layout by Kerry Ellis

CHAPTER 1
BUG CIRCUS

"What is it, Sassafras?" I crouched down and ruffled my cat's fluffy fur. He was trying to flip over a heavy, mossy rock with his paws. Something good was definitely under there.

I gently tipped the rock over on its side. Yes! I clapped my hands together. This rock *was* hiding a treasure. A billion roly-poly bugs!

OK . . . maybe not a *billion*. But at least twenty.

Sassafras took a step forward. "Meow?"

"No! Don't eat the bugs! That's gross."

My cat loves bugs as much as I do. But we love them for different reasons. I love to play with them. He loves to eat them.

Hmmm. Now I just needed to think of something super amazing to do with the roly-polies. I held one in my hand and its tiny feet tickled as it walked.

Sassafras trotted over to my pile of stuff and pawed at my Thinking Goggles.

"Ooh, good idea," I said as I put them on my head.

Most scientists wear goggles over their eyes, and I do too when I need to keep my eyes safe. But when I need to think of brilliant ideas, I wear my Thinking Goggles on top of my head. That way they're closer to my brain.

The roly-poly on my hand walked across a bridge I'd made by touching the tips of my two pointer fingers together.

"I've got it! Let's make a bug circus!"

I bent some thin twigs into hoops for the bugs to crawl through. Then I set up some small, round rocks for them to balance on. Next, I tied some grass on either end of a flat piece of bark to make a swing that I held low to the ground (in case any of my performers fell).

My favorite part was a tightrope I made by balancing a long twig between two flat rocks. One of the biggest roly-polies crawled up to the twig tightrope.

I got down on my elbows in the soft

grass to cheer him on. "Come on, little buggy! You can do it!"

Almost . . . almost. No! He tumbled into the grass. And then another one followed. The bigger roly-polies were having too much trouble. Hmmm. I carefully plucked the smallest of the roly-polies from the ground.

"OK, little guy. You might be the smallest, but I think you can do this. Show me what you've got!"

I placed the tiny roly-poly on one end of the twig. As he crawled along, I held my breath and didn't let it out until he was across.

He made it! I jumped up, cheered, and looked around for my mom. Then I remembered she was inside packing. I was so used to her being out here with me.

"Mom is gonna love this. Let's get her, Sassafras. Come on!"

I glanced over my shoulder just in time

to catch Sassafras creeping toward my circus performers.

"No way, kitty. You're coming with me. I do *not* trust you out here with my bugs. My new little friends are not snacks!"

Sassafras gave me a stinky look, but he gave in and followed me. As we got close to the house, I spotted my mom in the window. But she wasn't looking at us. She was looking at our old barn. And holding a photo.

CHAPTER 2
THE MYSTERY PHOTO

Sassafras and I burst into my mom's office. She jumped and quickly hid the photo under a pile of papers before smiling at us.

"Mom! Sassafras found a billion rolypolies under a rock in our yard. And I wasn't sure what to do with them, but then I used my Thinking Goggles. And we made a circus! With a tightrope and everything. Can you come see? Please?"

"That sounds wonderful, Zoey. I'm almost finished getting ready for this trip.

Give me five more minutes?"

I shrugged and leaned on her desk while Sassafras wove through my legs. I was trying to act like I didn't mind her leaving for a trip. But maybe I felt a little nervous about not seeing her for a whole week.

I was also curious about that photo she'd stashed away so quickly. As she packed, I poked at her papers and scootched them around. Whoa. *What* was that? A purple glow came from under a pile of papers. I pushed the top papers aside and gasped. In the photo was my mom when she was around my age. She was grinning with two missing teeth. With a purple frog on her head. That was *glowing.* I almost dropped the photo.

Mom glanced over her shoulder. "What is it?"

I held out the photo with a trembling hand. "This ... photo ... the frog ... it's glowing. How?"

My mom spun around so fast that some of the papers she was holding fell and scattered on the ground.

"You *see Pip?*"

Pip? Who was Pip? What on earth was going on?

CHAPTER 3
PIP

Mom was still frozen in place. She whispered, "I never thought . . . I was so sure I was the only one."

She finally snapped out of it and sat down at her desk. "Sorry for acting strange. Come sit, and I'll try to explain." Mom shook her head once more and smiled at me.

I sat down slowly. I was super confused. A glowing frog? That only my mom could see? My stomach flipped and flopped.

I picked up Sassafras and gave him a squeeze. He settled into my lap and purred, which calmed me down a little. I seriously hoped that all of this would start making sense soon.

"Remember how this used to be Grandma and Grandpa's house?"

I nodded slowly and kept petting Sassafras as my heart thumped loudly.

"When I was your age, I also spent hours wandering in the forest. One day, I was tossing rocks into the stream when I saw something shimmer in the sunlight."

"The purple frog?" I guessed.

Mom nodded. "His bright purple skin was covered head to toe with neon-orange spots. I'd never seen anything like it. I was sure I'd discovered a new species!"

I nodded again. I love frogs, and I'd never seen a frog that looked like that.

"The poor thing was crumpled on the ground, barely breathing. I knew it must be very sick or hurt. I had to help it. I carefully scooped it up and held it close. I found an old empty fish tank in our barn and got to work figuring out what was wrong. Books helped a little, but I needed to run some simple experiments, too.

"I used what I learned from the experiments to help the frog recover. Once he was better, I knew I had to return

him to the forest. I reached into his tank and he hopped right into my hand! As I lifted him out, something incredible happened. It was the craziest thing I'd ever seen . . ."

I could tell my mom was about to say something big. My mom is a scientist, so she sees crazy things all the time. If this was the *craziest thing she'd ever seen*, then it must be incredible.

I leaned in, scooting so far forward that Sassafras slid to the ground with a *whump*. I quickly scooped him back up. "What happened? What did you see?"

"The frog looked me in the eye, smiled, and said, 'Thank you!'"

I clapped my hand over my mouth.

What was going on? Was my mom playing a joke on me? She seemed pretty serious. But a talking frog? Really? It just couldn't be true!

"I was so shocked," my mom continued, "I almost tossed the poor frog into the air! 'Whoa!' he said. 'Steady there, little girl! Don't be afraid. My name is Pip. And I'm so grateful for all of your help.'"

Here I *had* to interrupt. "But Mom – this is *crazy*! Frogs. Can't. Talk."

Mom patted my knee. "That's what I thought at first too. But the frog kept

on talking. I wasn't dreaming. I wasn't imagining things. There really was a frog named Pip talking to me.

"My hands shook so much that I set Pip on a table for his own safety. He told me he'd been out past dark looking for something he'd dropped during the day. An owl attacked him. He was terrified and hurt, but managed to escape. He didn't remember anything after that until he woke up in our barn.

"Once I recovered from the shock of it all, Pip told me that there are lots of magical animals in our forests. Humans can't usually see them. He asked if I'd help others like him who were hurt or sick. I agreed, of course. Pip spread the word about me and the barn after he left. And I've been helping the magical animals of our forest ever since."

A big smile spread across my face. This was incredible. The only thing I might love more than science is magic. And my mom was telling me there was magic right here in our own backyard!

CHAPTER 4
THE DOORBELL

I was so excited. And had *so* many
questions.

"Why is purple light coming out of the
photo? Because of the magic? And how
come I've never seen any of the magical
creatures? They do still come here, right?
Where do you keep them? Are there some
here now?"

Mom laughed. "Phew! OK, let's see
here. Yes, the photo glows because of
the magic. Any time you photograph a

magical creature, some of the magic stays in the photo. When a magical animal does need my help, I keep it in our barn. And finally, no, there aren't any magical animals here right now. Sometimes no one needs my help for weeks at a time. This will all make more sense once I've shown you the barn. Come on."

As Mom and I walked out to the barn together, I laughed to myself. I never played there because I thought it was super boring. Boy, was I wrong.

Mom led me around to the back door of the barn. "Before he left for the forest, Pip added a special doorbell to our barn's

back door. I thought I was the only one in the family who could see it. But I'm guessing you'll be able to see it too."

Sassafras interrupted my mom by meowing loudly.

Mom laughed. "Oh yes, I should add that clever animals like Sassafras can see it as well."

I knelt down and looked all over the back wall of the barn. "But I don't see anything."

"Try lying down on your stomach.

Now a little to the left. And down just a tiny bit. Do you see it?"

The grass tickled my neck as I lowered my head a little more. All of a sudden, I could see a round button. It looked like a regular doorbell, except this one shimmered in a wave of rainbow colors. I moved my head up a bit and it disappeared. Whoa. No wonder I'd never noticed this before.

Although now that I thought about it,

I might have at least *heard* it before. Every once in a while the most beautiful tinkling sound would come from my mom's office. She always told me it was an alarm on her phone reminding her to do something. I guess I never thought to ask what.

"That bell that rings in our house sometimes? Is that the barn doorbell?"

"Yes, that's it. I never know when I'll hear the bell, but whenever I'm home, I'm always listening."

"What about when you're gone? What happens then?"

"Well, all I can do is hope that I'm here when the bell rings and an animal needs me."

I remembered my mom standing in the window, looking out at the barn. She must have been worried about what would happen while she was gone at this conference. Maybe . . . maybe I could help.

"You're going to be gone for a *week*. That's a long time. If an animal rings the bell while you're gone, do you think maybe I could help them?" I looked down at my feet and poked the ground with my toe. "I mean, I know I'm just a kid. But I could try."

My mom smiled. "I was hoping you'd suggest that. Are you sure? It might be a lot to handle. Though you could always call me if you needed help."

I nodded and stood up a little straighter. Mom put her hands on my shoulders and kissed my forehead.

"Now I won't have to worry while I'm gone. Thank you."

My stomach did flips. On one hand I was super excited to meet a magical animal. On the other hand, I was worried that I wouldn't know what to do. I didn't want to mess up.

But my mom was my age when she helped Pip. A kid had done this alone before.

Which meant I could handle it.

Right?

CHAPTER 5
THE BARN

Mom opened the door, and we stepped inside. The barn felt different. Magical. It was like I'd never seen it before. Now I knew it held secrets.

"These cabinets hold the medical supplies I've gathered over the years," Mom said. "And over here are some books that you might find helpful. There aren't any books about magical animals. But you'll find that magical creatures and everyday animals are often similar.

Once I had a sick winged fox, and it helped to read about both birds and foxes. Sometimes you'll need to run an experiment to figure out what the animal needs or what will work best. You can look through my old science journals over there to get a better idea of what I'm talking about."

My heart beat faster. As soon as she was done with the tour, I was heading straight for those journals. My breath caught. There'd be more magical photos in there! I could hardly wait to see them.

I interrupted her. "So if I hear the bell, I run out here? And the animal will be at the back door? And I bring it inside and try to figure out what's wrong?"

Mom nodded. "Some of the animals can speak, like Pip, but most can't. Remember, you can use the books and my old journals to help you. This must seem like a lot of responsibility. But I know you'll do your best. Do you have any questions?"

My mind was spinning, but I shook my head no. If Mom believed I could handle this, I could. I hoped.

And if things got too tricky, I could ask Dad to help. Wait a minute. Mom hadn't mentioned Dad at all. That was definitely strange.

"What about Dad? Can't he help me?"

"Your father can't see any of the magical animals. Until you saw Pip in that photo, I thought I was the only human who could see them." Mom shook her head sadly. "I tried to introduce Pip to your Dad once, but he couldn't see or hear him."

Whoa. So this was definitely all up to me.

Mom kissed me on the head. "I've got to go. But I'll see you in a week! I'll let Dad know you're out here before I leave."

"Wait!" I piped up. "If a magical creature comes, do I get to take its picture?" I was pretty sure that one of the best parts of this whole thing was going to be collecting magic photos.

Mom laughed and opened one of the desk drawers. "Here's my camera. You're free to use it – but since it's instant film, you can't take too many photos or it'll get really expensive. Only take one of each animal, OK? Oh, and here." She dug around at the bottom of the drawer. "A brand new science journal, just for you."

I wrapped my arms around my mom
and gave her a big squeeze. I was glad

to have the stuff in all the cabinets and drawers *and* Mom's old science journals to distract me. It made saying good-bye much easier.

I set my Thinking Goggles on the barn desk and grabbed the pile of science notebooks. I spent the next few hours with Sassafras curled up in my lap as I flipped through all of them. The photos were *so* incredible. I flipped to a page with a creature that looked like a flower. I leaned in for a closer look, and the scent of roses filled my nose.

A few pages later I found a photo of something fluffy and blue that was shaped like a snake. I brushed my fingers over the photo and I could feel its soft feathers. This was going to be so much fun. I could hardly wait to see what creature I'd get to meet first.

CHAPTER 6

THE DOORBELL

RINGS

The next day I stayed right by mom's office, listening. Nothing happened. The day after was the same. Not a peep from the bell. But on the fifth day, there I was reading on the couch when, at long last, I heard the magical tinkling sound. I popped up so fast, I catapulted Sassafras out of my lap.

He went flying through the air and let out a yelp, but landed on his feet. Sassafras gave me a grumpy stare, but then his ears turned toward the bell. He heard it too! We both darted for the barn. We couldn't wait to see who needed our help.

At the back door of the barn, I paused to listen. It was completely silent. Except for the pounding of my heart. I grinned down at Sassafras. "Ready, kitty?"

He meowed and pawed at the door. I took that as a yes.

I slowly opened the door to find a small, green, scaly animal curled up in a tight ball. I heard a rustling in the bushes and glanced up in time to see a shimmery blue tail disappear into the forest. Maybe another animal had brought this one here for help?

"Hello?" I called out. But nothing answered, and the mysterious blue animal didn't come back.

I gently reached down to touch the smooth green back of the little creature curled up at my feet. As I did, a tiny head peeped up. "Oh!" I whispered. "You are so cute."

Two sad eyes stared up at me.

"Don't worry, little guy. We'll make you feel better!" I scooped him into my arms. Sassafras anxiously wove between my legs as I carried the animal into the barn.

I set him down on a wood table. "You're kinda heavy for such a little thing." I gave him one more gentle pet. He slowly stretched, and two little wings and a long tail popped out. He was a dragon! And he was so tiny, he just had to be a baby.

A baby dragon! In my barn!

"Hey, little guy. What's wrong? I don't see any scrapes or cuts. But you wouldn't be at the barn if you didn't need help." He seemed pretty weak. After looking around, he dropped his head down to the table and just lay there.

Sassafras hopped onto the table and gave the dragon a good sniffing. The baby dragon's head popped up, and he let out a little cough. A spark flew out! Sassafras shot through the air and landed on the ground with all his fur standing on end.

Yikes! I needed to move this guy

before he coughed again.

"Hmmm. I need to find a place to keep you that won't catch on fire." I looked around the barn. "Let's see . . . wood, fabric, and hay all burn easily. Bingo! Let's put you in this pen with a dirt floor. If you cough again, the dirt won't catch fire."

Phew. Tucking the baby under my arm, I quickly moved him to the pen. Sassafras hung back and watched us from outside the pen. My kitty was no longer so sure he wanted to cozy up to our new friend!

CHAPTER 7
HATCHING
SNAKES

Now that I was pretty sure our barn wasn't going to burst into flames, I needed to help the dragon. His tiny body lay there like a little lump. Poor thing!

I circled him a few times. At first I thought he might have a cold, but he didn't cough again. I flipped through my mom's science journals. There weren't any entries on dragons. I was stumped. I set the journals on the desk, which knocked my Thinking Goggles to the ground. Perfect!

I dusted them off and popped them onto my head.

I could feel a memory tickling my brain right away. Something that had happened last summer? Something with the forest? That was it!

Last summer Mom and I were on a walk. Sassafras (who never missed a good

hike) stopped in his tracks by a pile of
rocks. He wouldn't budge. Mom knelt
down to see what was so captivating.

"Zoey! Do you see the little head
peeking out of that egg? These snake eggs
are hatching. Let's watch!"

Each little snake head pushed and
pushed until *boom!* Its egg burst open and
a baby snake slithered out. Most of them

barely rested before skittering off into the forest.

We watched until only one egg was left. The little snake inside was having a really tough time. Once he popped out, he lay there without moving. He was so much smaller than his brothers and sisters.

"What's wrong with him?" I looked around. "Where is their mother? Why isn't she helping them?"

"Snakes aren't mammals like us. They're reptiles. They have scales, and the mother snake laid eggs. Remember how reptiles rarely take care of their babies?"

I did remember reading that, but now that I was seeing it in person, it seemed cruel. "But they're so tiny! They can't take care of themselves. How will they know what to do?"

"Even though they're small, they're born ready to take care of themselves. They know how to hunt to feed themselves and how to hide to keep themselves safe."

I looked down at the tiny, weak snake. "What will happen to this one? He's so small." I frowned. "He seems sick."

"When animals have a lot of babies at once, sometimes there are a few that aren't as big or as strong as the rest. Some people call them runts. I'm sorry to say it, but they usually don't survive."

A tear rolled down my cheek. Staring down at that tiny little snake and thinking of him dying was just too sad.

Mom gave my shoulder a squeeze. "Why don't we give this snake a little help? We could make his first meal nice and easy. It might give him a boost. Many baby snakes like to eat worms . . ."

Before my mom could finish her

sentence, I was furiously digging. I am a champion worm finder. Within a minute, I found a good-sized one. I felt a little bad, because I kind of love worms, but we handed him over. Mom gently wiggled the worm in front of the baby snake, and he perked up. He swallowed the worm in one big gulp. Sassafras yelped as the little snake came to life and bolted into the bushes.

I patted my Thinking Goggles. That was it! Maybe this baby dragon was the runt of his litter. Maybe he was *hungry*. I'd solved it! All I had to do was get him some...

Wait. What do dragons eat?

CHAPTER 8
THE FOOD EXPERIMENT

All this thinking about food made me hungry. My stomach gurgled loudly. Sassafras growled.

"Silly Sassafras!" I ruffled his fur. "I'm just hungry for lunch. Let's go back to the house."

As we walked, I realized I had a great question for an experiment. I grabbed my brand new science journal and sat down with my sandwich. On the first page, I wrote:

QUESTION: what do baby dragons like to eat?

Hmmm. The baby dragon had scales like that little snake. I bet he was a reptile. If snakes ate worms, maybe dragons did too. Sure, this baby dragon was a lot bigger than the baby snake in the forest. So maybe he'd eat a *lot* of worms.

I knew I should try several different kinds of foods, just in case. I worried it might be hard to get the baby dragon to eat, so I picked some of my favorites. I set my choices on the kitchen table and wrote them all down.

MATERIALS:

worms

apple slices

eggs

cheese

marshmallows

cereal

granola bar

Now to make a guess. I would eat the marshmallows, but that baby snake ate the worm as if it tasted like a marshmallow. I shrugged. Maybe worms were like the reptile version of marshmallows?

HYPOTHESIS: I think he will eat worms. (Sorry, Worms)

Now I needed to set up my experiment. Every time I'm experimenting, my mom always tells me the exact same thing: "Remember to change only *one* thing, and keep everything else in your experiment the same." And by every time, I really mean she says it *every* time.

I wanted to change the kind of food I was giving him, so I needed to keep everything else the same. I got seven of the *same* white plates out of our cabinet. I measured out the *same* amount of each kind of food – one kind of food per plate. I grinned. This experiment would make my mom happy.

MATERIALS:

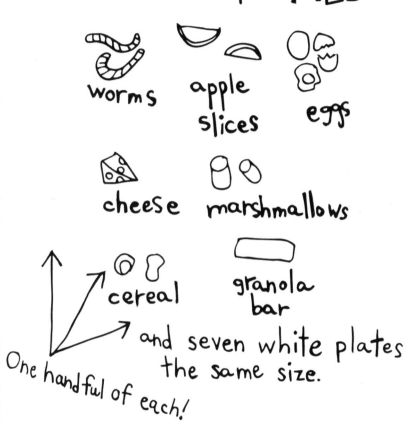

worms

apple slices

eggs

cheese

marshmallows

cereal

granola bar

One handful of each!

and seven white plates the same size.

Next I decided what my steps would be.

1. Set one handful of each food on each plate at the same distance from the baby dragon.
2. Step out of the pen and watch him.
3. Write down what he eats.

All set! I gathered my supplies in my arms and tucked my science notebook under my chin.

When Sassafras and I got to the barn, I was surprised to see that the dragon was looking around a bit. "Hey, little guy," I said softly. "I've got some foods here for you to try!"

I set each plate of food the same distance away from the dragon. He watched me with big, curious eyes. Once everything was in place, I stepped out of the pen to take notes. The baby dragon got up and carefully licked the food on the first plate. The cereal stuck to his tongue! He scrunched up his face, jumped back, and pawed at his tongue. Whoops!

I made a quick note in my journal:

Dragons do not like cereal.

Once he wiped off all the cereal pieces,
he calmed down. Then his nostrils got
really wide. He sniffed and took a few
steps, then sniffed some more. He skipped
all the other plates and went straight to
the marshmallows. His little blue tongue
shot out for a lick, and his eyes lit up. He
was so excited, he let out a little hiccup.
A spark landed on the marshmallow and
smoked a bit before going out. The dragon
immediately gobbled up the toasted
marshmallow.

I had to giggle – roasted
marshmallows are the best! I bet he would
really like s'mores! I wrote down my
conclusion:

Dragons love marshmallows!

As Sassafras and I watched him cough out a spark to toast each of the marshmallows that were left, I made a decision.

I looked down at Sassafras. "We need to call him something other than 'little guy.'" I grinned. "Let's call him Marshmallow!" Sassafras purred in agreement.

A few minutes later, Marshmallow was running and hopping around the pen, flapping his little wings as he jumped into the air. I couldn't stop laughing. Eating a whole plate of marshmallows would make me feel the same way!

Sassafras couldn't resist the fun and joined Marshmallow in the pen. The two of them played and played until they fell into a fluffy, scaly heap. Sassafras was panting a bit so I brought a big bowl of water to the pen. They eagerly drank with their heads side by side. Then Marshmallow settled down in the dirt. He tucked his tail in, rested his head on top,

and closed his eyes.

"Time for another nap, huh?"
Marshmallow didn't make a peep.

Through the barn windows, I
could see that the sky was getting dark.
"Sassafras!" I whispered. "Time for dinner!
Let's leave Marshmallow to sleep for the
night. We'll see him in the morning."

As Sassafras and I tiptoed out of the

barn, I spotted the camera. Oh man, I couldn't wake the little guy now. And I wanted his sweet face in the photo. I'd have to take the picture the next morning.

When I got back to the house, my dad was at the stove, cooking. I grinned when I saw what he was making. Sassafras-shaped pancakes. A Dad specialty. He makes it look easy, but it isn't. My mom and I have tried to make them, but our pancakes end up looking like weird blobs.

Dad looked up and smiled at my Thinking Goggles, still perched on my head. "Whatcha been working on?" he asked.

I almost told him about Marshmallow. But then I remembered how he couldn't see magical creatures. I figured I'd better leave out the details about the baby dragon.

"Just some science experiments with Sassafras out in the barn."

Dad flipped another pancake. "That's

great, honey. I'm so glad you two have been able to keep yourselves busy with your mom gone."

Oh, we were keeping ourselves busy all right. If Dad only knew!

I could hardly wait for morning to come. First, I'd get my magical photo of that sweet little face. Then I'd spend the whole day playing . . . with a baby dragon!

CHAPTER 9
SASSAFRAS?

I woke up early and reached out to give Sassafras his morning snuggle. His usual spot by my feet was cold and empty. I sat up and looked around my room. No Sassafras.

"Sassafras?" I hollered. "Sassafras?"

Still nothing. He was always here when I woke up. Where could he be? He had to be around here somewhere.

Maybe he went out to the barn? I quickly threw on a jacket and a hat. It sure was cold out.

I opened the barn door and called out, "Sassafras? Are you in here?"

Instead of running to greet me, I heard him meow from Marshmallow's pen.

I peeked at them. "Sassafras! You scared me. What are you doing in here? Were you missing Marshmallow, sweet boy?" I held out my hand, expecting Sassafras to come over for his morning cuddles. But he wouldn't budge from the dragon's side.

I got closer and put a hand down to pet both Sassafras and Marshmallow. As soon as my hand

touched Marshmallow's back, I jumped.
He was like a block of ice! Why was he
so cold? And he wasn't moving. Oh no!
Something was really wrong.

And then it hit me. Our little dragon
was a reptile. How could I have forgotten
that reptiles can't make their own heat?

I jumped to my feet in search of a

heater. Thankfully, the third cabinet I looked in had one. I let out a big sigh of relief. I plugged it in and set it in the pen facing the dragon.

I should have remembered this! Only a few months ago, my friend Sophie went on vacation. She had just gotten the sweetest little baby lizard as a pet. I was over-the-

moon excited to watch him while she was gone.

When she brought him over, this big lamp thing was resting on top of his terrarium. Sophie told me it was his heat lamp, and she made me pinky promise to be really careful about always leaving it on. I thought that was weird, so I asked her why. "He needs something to make him warm all the time. He's cold-blooded, so he can't do it himself," she told me. "If you don't plug in the lamp, he can get really sick — or die!"

After Sophie left, I asked my mom to tell me more about what being cold-blooded meant. "Reptiles are cold-blooded," Mom told me. "Mammals like Sassafras and us keep warm using energy from the food we eat. We can even keep ourselves the same temperature by sweating when we are too hot and shivering when we are too cold. We are *warm-blooded* animals.

"But reptiles like Sophie's lizard can't use food energy to keep themselves warm," she continued. "Reptiles can't shiver to warm themselves up either. They are *cold-blooded* animals. In the mornings, you can often spot cold-blooded animals warming their bodies with heat from the sun. Once they're warm enough, they slither, crawl, or hop away! At night and in

the winter, they find caves or burrows or other animals to huddle up with to keep warm. It's important to keep pet reptiles at a safe temperature using something like a heat lamp."

Good thing Mom had a little heater out here in the barn! Now that the pen was nice and warm, the baby dragon started moving a bit. He picked up his head. Phew. I let out a breath I hadn't realized I'd been holding.

Marshmallow took a few more steps, then stumbled and fell to the ground. He didn't get up. I fixed the temperature. I fed him the night before. What could be going on?

He let out a heartbreaking whimper and half closed his eyes. Oh no! Was he dying? I didn't know what to do. My heart pounded. I walked one way, then another. I needed something . . . I needed my *mom!*

CHAPTER 10
THE CALL

I ran into the house. At first I went to get my dad, but then I remembered he couldn't help. I took a shaky breath. Then I grabbed the phone and called my mom.

I tried not to cry while the phone rang. The call went to voicemail. I couldn't hold it in anymore. Tears ran down my face. The dragon was going to die, and it was all my fault.

My dad came running. "Zoey? What's wrong? Are you hurt?"

I wasn't sure what to say that would make sense. Finally, I choked out, "I really need to talk to Mom, but she isn't

answering."

My dad hugged me and sat down with his arm around me. "You're really missing her, aren't you?"

I nodded and tried to stop crying.

"She's presenting at the conference right now, so her phone must be turned off. Why don't you leave a message? I'm sure she'll call you as soon as the talk is over."

Oh no! Mom's talk! It might be hours before she turned her phone back on. And by then it might be too late. I cried harder.

"I know I'm not Mom, but could I try to help? Can you tell me what made you so upset?"

If I told Dad about Marshmallow, he wouldn't understand at all. But maybe he could help me with the problem anyway?

"I was running an experiment where I fed a creature I found in the barn. It ate a bunch of one of the foods I gave it yesterday. And it looked really good when

I came in last night. But this morning it seems really sick. It's barely moving. I don't know what's wrong with it."

Dad frowned a bit. "It's not a wild animal, is it? That could be dangerous. Maybe I should come take a look."

"No, it's not really a wild animal. It's more of a, um, creature. Mom said it was OK. And, uh, I don't think you'd really be able to see it."

Dad looked confused. "Is it another one of your bug experiments? I hope it's not a spider. I really don't like spiders."

I shook my head no.

"I'm glad you checked with Mom first. Hmmm. Maybe the food you fed it was a little rough on it? Remember how awful you felt when we went camping last summer and you ate way too many s'mores?"

S'mores. Marshmallows. Too many marshmallows. Maybe that was it! My science experiment showed me what the baby dragon *liked* to eat, but maybe not what he *should* eat.

What had my parents done to make me feel better last summer? That was one of the worst stomachaches ever. Let's see, Mom lectured me about eating too much sugar. And she had me drink a lot of water. And eat a really healthy meal that had no sugar.

I needed to get Marshmallow some water and some healthy food right away! I jumped up and dashed to the door. Then I stopped, ran back, and gave my dad a big hug. "Thanks, Dad! I think I know how to fix it!"

CHAPTER 11
WHAT SHOULD BABY DRAGONS EAT?

Marshmallow was sleeping when I got to the barn. I filled up his water dish and quietly set it near him. What foods would be healthy for a baby dragon? Mom had said that studying normal animals that might be related to the magical creatures had helped her before. Like when she had the winged fox that was sick. She'd read about foxes and birds to figure out what to do.

I ran to the bookshelf. My eyes quickly scanned the books. Bingo! I grabbed *Care*

and *Feeding of Reptiles* from the second shelf. The chapter on reptile diets had just what I needed.

> *Your pet reptile is either a carnivore, an omnivore, or an herbivore and should be fed accordingly. If your reptile is a carnivore, offer a source of meat. Some carnivorous reptiles prefer animal meat, such as mice or fish.*

Other carnivorous reptiles prefer smaller sources of meat, such as earthworms or crickets. If your reptile is an herbivore, offer a plant source, such as leafy greens or vegetables. If your reptile is an omnivore, it will eat some meat foods and some plant foods.

There was no time to waste. I needed to figure out whether Marshmallow was a carnivore, an herbivore, or both – an omnivore!

As I ran to the house for supplies, I pushed down my worries. I had to believe that this experiment would help. Hang on, baby dragon!

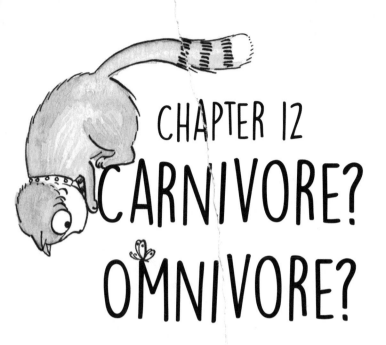

CHAPTER 12
CARNIVORE?
OMNIVORE?

I darted around the kitchen. I needed some kind of animal meat. I opened the fridge. Yes! I'd forgotten that Dad had gone fishing with his friends a few days before. He always saves a few of the smallest fish as treats for Sassafras. I grabbed two fish.

"Hey, Sassafras. Can you share one of these with Marshmallow?"

Sassafras stared at both fish and meowed loudly. He grabbed one, dropped it in his food bowl, and took a bite.

That left me with one fish. I figured
that counted as permission to share it
with the baby dragon. I didn't wait to
see if Sassafras would change his mind. I
quickly gathered the other things I needed
for the experiment and went straight to
the barn with Sassafras at my heels.

If Marshmallow ate either the fish or
the worms but ignored the plants, he was
probably a carnivore. If he ate just the

plants, he was probably an herbivore. And if he ate both meat and plants, he was probably an omnivore. I knew I should be writing all of this in my journal, but it would have to wait until later. Little Marshmallow needed me to be quick.

He was still lying there, slumped on the ground and barely awake. I didn't think he'd make it over to the plates, so I put them all right in front of him. Sassafras meowed and stared at the fish longingly. I picked him up and petted him. It gave my nervous hands something to do.

I waited. Nothing happened. Little Marshmallow was too weak! I snuggled Sassafras and tried to think. What could I do? Maybe I should put the food right up to his mouth?

I dangled some worms in front of him and wiggled them. "Want a little taste?"

Marshmallow took a lick, and then laid his head back down.

I tried the same thing with each of the
other foods. He gave them all one lick,
but he didn't eat any of them. I sat on the
ground and put my head in my hands. I
couldn't even watch anymore.

Then I heard a sound. I looked up to
see Marshmallow crawling over to the fish.
He swallowed the whole thing in one gulp.

Then he tucked his tail under his head and closed his eyes and went to sleep. I crossed my fingers and toes that the fish and the nap would do the trick. It was breaking my heart to see little Marshmallow so sick.

Sassafras bumped my chin with his head and purred. He could tell that I was super worried about Marshmallow.

I decided to read through the rest of
the reptile book, just in case there was
something I'd missed. Sassafras curled up
in my lap like a warm, rumbling blanket
as I read.

CHAPTER 13
MOM!

My eyes flew open and I looked around. The reptile book had fallen out of my hands. Sassafras quietly snored on my chest. I must've fallen asleep while I was reading.

I heard my dad calling my name. Huh? Was it dinnertime already? Sassafras and I ran into the house and looked around, confused.

"Is it time for dinner?"

Dad laughed. "Did you forget that your

mom was coming home today?"

"Mom's back? Mom's back! *Mom!*" I ran to her office, hugged her, and then burst into tears.

"I messed everything up! There was a baby dragon and I wasn't sure what was wrong. I fed him marshmallows, and at first he got better, but then he got so much worse. I tried to fix it by feeding him fish. But I don't know if it worked. I don't want him to die!" I sobbed.

My mom knelt down and looked me in the eye. "Oh, Zoey. You must've been very worried. But magical animals are much tougher than you think. Let's go see how he's doing."

CHAPTER 14
BIGGER

Mom walked me out to the barn with her arm around me. I had hoped I could handle all of this on my own. I wanted to impress my mom with a healthy dragon. Instead she was going to see a sick dragon that I hadn't been able to help.

We walked into the barn and I stopped. I rubbed my eyes. "Whoa."

Marshmallow was walking around. He had bright eyes. And he was at least twice as big as he'd been this morning! How did

that happen? Dragons must grow *really* quickly.

Sassafras was about to walk into the pen, but froze. I think he was also shocked to see how big our little guy had gotten!

Marshmallow trotted over and nuzzled Sassafras, who purred loudly. The two of them jumped around and played while I stared in awe.

Mom squeezed me in a big hug. "Zoey, I'm so proud. You kept trying

even when things got hard. How about we leave these two to play and see if we can convince your dad to part with some more fish?"

Just like that, the day went from awful to wonderful. I did it! Even though I made some mistakes along the way, I helped Marshmallow.

CHAPTER 15
LEARNING TO FISH

Sassafras and I were out in the barn playing with Marshmallow. Only a few days had passed, but Marshmallow was about the size of a horse. Sassafras liked to jump on his back between his wings. Then Marshmallow would run in circles around the pen until Sassafras started to fall and jumped off. Marshmallow always stopped to sniff and make sure Sassafras was all right. I wanted to remember the way they played together forever. Oh! I'd never

taken my photo of Marshmallow. I dashed
off to get the camera and got an action
shot of the two of them together.

Mom came into the barn and looked
at the photo of Sassafras
riding

Marshmallow. At first
she laughed a lot, but then she got quiet.

"Marshmallow's getting awfully big, Zoey."

I sucked in a big breath. I knew what she was going to say next, and I didn't want to hear it.

"I know this part is hard. But a dragon isn't meant to live in a barn. He's meant to be free!"

I nodded and kept looking down. If I looked up at Marshmallow, I was sure I'd start crying. "I guess he'd have more fun flying around and exploring the forest," I mumbled. "And he might not even fit in the barn much longer."

Saying good-bye was going to stink.

Once Sassafras was done dragon-riding, we all headed for the forest stream. Mom wanted to teach Marshmallow how to catch fish.

When we got to the stream, Marshmallow seemed nervous. Rather than check out the stream, he snuggled up behind me and put his big head on my

shoulder. Sassafras hates getting wet, so he
hid behind Marshmallow.

Mom rolled up her pants and splashed
around in the water. "Marshmallow, the
stream won't hurt you. It's really fun.
See?" After a few minutes, Marshmallow's
curiosity got the best of him. He joined her
in the water.

Next she showed him that there were
fish in the stream. Once he realized that, he
really loved
the stream.
He spotted
a fish in the
water and
tried
to

catch it, but he missed and ended up with a mouthful of stream water.

"Don't give up, Marshmallow! You can do it!" Sassafras and I cheered.

Marshmallow kept trying and finally caught one. After that first taste of success, he got much faster at catching fish. He even brought a little fish to Sassafras, who purred loudly in thanks.

I was rolling up my pants to join the fun when Sassafras started meowing like crazy. He stared at the bushes nearby.

I stood very still and watched. A blue dragon head slowly peeped out of the bushes. It looked about the same size as Marshmallow.

"Come on, sweet girl," I cooed. The dragon kept her eyes on me as she took a few small steps forward.

The splashing behind us stopped. I looked over my shoulder, and Marshmallow and my mom were both frozen, watching the new dragon. Then

Marshmallow let out the most beautiful sound. It sounded like a cat's purr, only louder and more like a song. Maybe dragons purr when they're really happy?

The new dragon's eyes lit up and she purred right back! She trotted into the stream and sniffed Marshmallow. They twisted their necks around each other in greeting and purred even more.

Something about the way her blue tail moved was so familiar. Was she the friend who had brought baby Marshmallow to our barn and disappeared into the bushes?

The blue dragon took a few steps toward the forest. She looked back and called out to Marshmallow. She wanted him to come with her.

My heart dropped. I was going to have to say good-bye to my dragon.

Marshmallow took a step to follow her, then stopped. He came bounding over to us and nuzzled my mom and Sassafras. Then he rested his head on my shoulder. I wrapped my arms around his warm, strong neck.

I blinked back tears. "Good-bye, Marshmallow. Be a good dragon."

I gave him a gentle nudge toward the

new dragon. He
looked at me one last time.

"Go ahead. It's OK." I waved him on.

Before I could change my mind, they
both leapt into the air. The forest filled
with the beautiful noise of two happy
dragons. The sound was so pretty that it
was hard to be sad.

My mom moved to my side and
wrapped me in a hug. "Look how healthy
and happy he is. That's because of *your*
help."

I nodded and couldn't help but smile
as I watched them spin and dive through
the air until they were nothing more than
specks in the sky.

CHAPTER 16
SMOKE?

I cleaned out Marshmallow's pen while Sassafras watched. It looked so empty without our little dragon bounding around. Even Sassafras was mopey. We all really missed Marshmallow.

I sniffed back another wave of tears. Wait a minute. I sniffed again.

"Do you smell smoke, Sassafras? Where's it coming from?"

Sassafras pawed at the barn door and meowed. Oh no, was something burning outside? We burst out of the barn to find my mom standing by a fire in our backyard fire pit. She held two sticks and a bag of marshmallows.

She smiled. "Roasted marshmallows seemed like an appropriate way to celebrate your success with our dragon friend."

We cuddled up by the fire telling stories about the little guy and laughing. I ate five or six

marshmallows, and went to grab another one. But then I remembered how Marshmallow felt after eating the plate of marshmallows. I set my roasting stick down and just enjoyed the fire. I'd skip the stomachache!

After we headed in for the night, I went to my bedroom. Sassafras jumped up on my desk and nosed at my science notebook. It fell open to the next blank page.

I laughed and snuggled him up. "Oh, Sassafras, I know how you feel. I can't wait to meet our next magical friend either!"

GLOSSARY

Carnivore: An animal that eats only meat

Cold-blooded: An animal that uses the sun to warm up and shade to cool itself because it can't control its body temperature

Conclusion: What you learned from your experiment (hopefully you get an answer to your question but sometimes you don't)

Herbivore: An animal that eats only plants

Hypothesis: What you think will happen in your experiment

Omnivore: An animal that eats plants and meat

Reptile: An animal that has scales and is cold-blooded

Warm-blooded: An animal that doesn't need the sun to warm up or shade to cool itself because it can control its body temperature

ABOUT THE AUTHOR AND ILLUSTRATOR

ASIA CITRO used to be a science teacher, but now she plays at home with her two kids and writes books. When she was little, she had a cat just like Sassafras. He loved to eat bugs and always made her laugh (his favorite toy was a plastic human nose that he carried everywhere). Asia has also written three activity books: *150+ Screen-Free Activities for Kids, The Curious Kid's Science Book,* and *A Little Bit of Dirt.* She has yet to find a baby dragon in her backyard, but she always keeps an eye out, just in case.

MARION LINDSAY is a children's book illustrator who loves stories and knows a good one when she reads it. She likes to draw anything and everything but does spend a completely unfair amount of time drawing cats. Sometimes she has to draw dogs just to make up for it. She illustrates picture books and chapter books as well as painting paintings and designing patterns. Like Asia, Marion is always on the lookout for dragons and sometimes thinks there might be a small one living in the airing cupboard.

for activities and more visit
ZOEYANDSASSAFRAS.COM